CW00504807

FIRST STORY
CHANGING LIVES THROUGH WRITING

First Story changes lives through writing.

There is dignity and power in telling our own story. We help disadvantaged young people find their voices.

First Story places professional writers into secondary schools serving low-income communities, where they work intensively with students and teachers to foster confidence, creativity and writing ability.

Our programmes expand young people's horizons and raise aspirations. Students gain vital skills that underpin their success in school and support their transition to further education and employment.

To find out more and get involved, go to www.firststory.org.uk.

First Story is a registered charity number 1122939 and a private company limited by guarantee incorporated in England with number 06487410. First Story is a business name of First Story Limited.

First published 2019 by First Story Limited
Omnibus Business Centre, 39–41 North Road, London, N7 9DP

www.firststory.org.uk

ISBN 978-0-85748-399-7

1 3 5 7 9 10 8 6 4 2

A CIP catalogue record for this book is available from the British Library.

Printed and bound in the UK by Aquatint
Typeset by Avon DataSet Ltd
Copyedited by Emily Bedford
Proofread by Gemma Harris
Cover designed by Fiona MacColl at Oxford University Press

Peach Juice
& Problems

An Anthology by the First Story Group
at Pimlico Academy

EDITED BY STEVEN CAMDEN | 2019

FIRST STORY
CHANGING LIVES THROUGH WRITING

As Patron of First Story I am delighted that it continues to foster and inspire the creativity and talent of young people in secondary schools serving low-income communities.

I firmly believe that nurturing a passion for reading and writing is vital to the health of our country. I am therefore greatly encouraged to know that young people in this school – and across the country – have been meeting each week throughout the year in order to write together.

I send my warmest congratulations to everybody who is published in this anthology.

Camilla

HRH The Duchess of Cornwall

Contents

Introduction

Steven Camden, Writer-in-Residence

Secondary school is chaos.

Anyone stepping onto site from the outside world will tell you, it's like walking onto a movie set pitched as *Carnival meets The Occupy Movement meets Bull Run meets Job Interview*.

Those experienced teachers and students who tread the corridors daily do so by way of a seasoned navigation, rather than any kind of innocent wandering. The swirling tornado of Years Seven to Sixth Form will swallow you up and spit you out somewhere in the future.

Pimlico Academy is no different.

Each Wednesday afternoon as I came to reception, touch-typed my name and the name of Harriet Lacey into the LCD display and stood awkwardly waiting for the lowest resolution webcam to take a grainy silhouette photograph of my head, I could sense the bubbling energy of commotion just beyond that first key-locked door into the school.

And let me tell you why I loved it.

I loved it because it felt the same as I remember. I remember standing in corridors dressed in my hand-me-down blazer and pin-tucked trousers, feeling like a pebble caught in a tidal wave. I remember the ten-times-a-day pendulum-swing of emotions from death row to blissful utopia and back again. Heartbreak and double Science. Peach juice and problems.

Each time Harriet would collect me, and we'd weave through shoals of students to our designated English classroom, I would feel myself filling with memories and emotions and ideas and, each time, our First Story participants flooded into that room filled with all of those same things and more.

The range of personalities and voices, of tones and interests, opinions and experience, has been the broadest I've encountered in all my First Story years.

As the students gathered around our long table and tucked into the biscuits and satsumas Harriet always kindly provided, you could physically feel a room full of people decompressing from the stresses of their day.

The mix of first-timers and First Story veterans gave the room a real family feel that let everyone kick off their shoes (sometimes literally) and dive into stories and discussions that felt safe and open, whilst also being challenging and contentious.

I am always keen to respond to a group rather than prescribe my own agenda for a session. I try to offer provocations that I think will excite them and which they haven't necessarily faced in their writing, and some of my exercises are a little tangential. This group of writers took up every challenge, ran with every prompt, investigated every oblique turn I threw at them and moulded their responses to suit their own voice and lens on the world.

The resulting pieces of work felt like the most gorgeous chaos. Poems. Songs. Characters. Free associations and slices of larger stories that I feel represent this group better than anything more 'structured' could do.

Reading the pieces back as I compiled the manuscript, I can feel the personality of each student breathing through each piece and page and I can picture each of their faces, speaking their words on a Wednesday afternoon around our long table, as the rest of us listened and shared in their ideas.

Secondary School is chaos, and Pimlico Academy is definitely the most Secondary-Schooliest Secondary School I've ever held residency in.

And it has been a complete pleasure.

Foreword

Harriet Lacey, English Teacher

Despite producing writing each week in the First Story workshops, I always find it difficult to condense the year into a short foreword and to adequately express thanks to First Story, our author, Steven, and the students who join us.

First Story is the highlight of my week and, as Steven and I wade through, against the flow of students leaving school, we know we will greet our group, who are already set up, chatting and munching, waiting to write. A group who often stay to chat afterwards and share some more of their personal writing with Steven, who seems to always have time to listen. Steven leaves an immense impression of generosity and kindness, with his energy and honest joy at each written creation, and an ability to, like the act of writing itself, be an architect of assurance in each student.

We've been a messy, slightly undisciplined and candid group this year, enjoying the exploration, numerous changes in direction and the freedom to break away from the full stop and the order of a lined, A4, portrait-orientation page. Which makes producing an anthology very interesting.

The final result is a credit to each student and Steven, and wouldn't have been possible without the hard work, patience and commitment of everyone at First Story, so thank you to everyone involved. I hope that our students go on to always write such beautiful chaos.

Red

Ayah

Flames in a fire
Flag for a bull
The meaning of blood
The symbol of rage
Breathing too fast
Knowing you're right
Purely redundant
On your own
Ambulance sirens
Incorrect
Corner of eyes
Troubled child
The texture of poison
Idea of help
A plan of pain
The love you don't want

Invisibility

Iman

Invisibility
It sounds cool, like
Something out of a movie
Something that's not real
But is it so amazing if you live with people looking right
    through you   To be invisible.
To live in a world where even the people who sat next to you
    for two years don't know your name
And those people who do see you, are not worth being seen by?
But
Sometimes you can like it
To be invisible
To sit in a corner, pencil in hand and feel as if you have
    the power
The power to
Be invisible.

My Morning Schedule

Azim

It's always the same.

I wake up, get dressed, eat breakfast, leave the house, forget my bag, go back to get it and it's 8.19.

Time to teleport to school again, forget my pencil case as always, get referred, get home, shower, do my homework, time travel to the American Declaration of Independence, come back to the present and sleep, wake up in the middle of the night to go to the toilet, try and go back to sleep. I start thinking about my time/era:

'Life in the 65th century is so mundane!'

Untitled Love

Kayana

Wandering around the withered cave of their abandoned house.
It was unfair.

Why did she, of all people, go with him?   Why wasn't it me?

Praying for a way to die and see him just one more time. The only thing holding me back was not knowing if he was in hell or heaven and if I would be with him or if she'd be there to stop me again.

The long rivers streaming out of my eyes land silently on the scorched wooden floor.

Trying to see through the waterfalls over my eyes... PAUSE EVERYTHING.

It was H... Him!   I could really see him. His ghost hovering around as if he was still alive. Wiping my eyes, I started to walk slowly to him as if I was going to his funeral again. I stopped right in front of him. Face to face. I tried to touch him but I felt only ice.

I looked him up and down, head to toe, crying even more, hugging myself.

His chilled mouth came close to my ear then he whispered, 'Let go and be free.' He vanished and I fell to the floor,
gone as well.

Raining

Madalena

Hello these days I'm sad
Hello these days I'm stressed
Hello these days I cry
Hello I'm seeing red
It's only in my head
It's only in my head
It's only in my head

                                  It's raining

How far will this lie take us?
How long until it breaks us?
How long until it takes our soul
Changes and remakes us?
This lie that we're fine, but inside we're crying
So we just sit and watch our lives go by
Till the rain comes and takes us to die

                                  It's raining

I'm swimming in mud, I'm drowning in oil
Tell me where is the ground, the earth and the soil?
I'm done with all this, I'm cleansing my soul
Flying off in my spaceship, all systems are go
But I'm stuck. I can't leave the water
And I can't ask for help 'cause that'd just be awkward
And nobody will come in, come in to save me
'Cause I'm not close with nobody. Save me

                                  It's raining.

Everything is not the Way it Should Be

Reinhardas

The old me is gone, trapped inside the depression and the regret of my past selves.

Taking my joy pills and putting on my positive mask won't help me keep the misery and the stress locked away anymore...

They should be forgotten, but they keep on coming back; being optimistic is impossible now. The virus is extremely contagious and showing these terrible things I feel will affect many people I meet in a very negative way. Now only a shadow reflects my old self...

It's time to let it loose; the old me is gone, and the new me has arrived...

The Queue

Sarah

I walk to the back of the queue. I'm estimating it will take around twenty minutes until I get food

First step
My friends are talking some nonsense about Mario Kart
I look in front and see another queue forming
The queue of the pusher-inners
There is a deep sensation to snitch
I don't want to risk getting bullied though

Second step
My friends are in front of me
How did that happen?
They were behind me before
The supervisor looks away
The pusher-inners pour into the line
Well, I won't be moving for another few minutes
Look at my watch
I've got ten minutes to get to the front of the queue, eat my
    food, go to the toilet and get to class
NOT GONNA HAPPEN

Third step
I can see students eating chicken and chips
Yummy
Look away   Look away
I was starting to dribble.

LOVE IS IN EVERYONE, EVEN IN THE HANDS OF EVIL

Sonny

The forest sat in a place where trees reached the sky's limits.

A place where life, love and freedom were forbidden. One hundred square kilometres and only one source of life sat grooming its rough, spiky fur. A glint of grimace and hate in its eyes were enough for most to steer clear. But for someone who was a real observer, they would see something else in its eyes, something missing.

It would roam night and day through this dark forest in search of someone it could lay its eyes on for ever. Someone who had compassion for it.

four lines of truth

Jenni

sometimes i wanna feel alive. saturday night where everything
   feels just right never compares
to monday morning where, in the hour of silence, i lose myself.
   just lose myself. where
another word will just tear through my very being. saturday
   euphoria never compares to
wednesday blues where everything existing stings my heart,
   cold and true.

Us

Harriet

You'll never love someone in that way again
I knew, as I stared at her face, pixelated
by the 3,823 miles.
Stuck, away. After years of sporadic contact, now it becomes
     urgent,
a matter of the heart.
Nestled, beautiful, enlarged, light, free, diseased,
     unfathomable,
glorious.

Escape

Nina

A campfire in the woods
I go home and light the candle
The delicate flame sits on the wax stick
I remember watching the embers as my eyelids slowly close
I am asleep
I dream of the subtle glow of the fire underneath the logs
And how it reminds me of the circular blaze under the steel pot
I wish it was a cosy winter's night with the fire burning
And a hot chocolate in my cold hand.

5.40 a.m.

Lola

'*Tu sei l'uomo*'
I smile at the man in the shop
I am definitely not the man, but it's nice to imagine
Using my keys to open my peach juice, I dodge the cracks on
    the sidewalk
A car beeps
Traffic lights go green
                            tired
It's sweeter than usual, the peach juice
The lies
    I gulp it down
    I want another bottle
I want a factory-full

Lambeth Bridge at dusk
What a time to be alive
The river's browner than usual
                         still tired
And I keep coming back to the same point
Everything
Is repeating
I want something new
No
I want something old
Something past
                    something I used to love
Someone
My hopes choke me

So
I drink from my peach juice

repeat.

THE GIRL IN THE SHADOWS

Aseel

They don't know she is living in pain,
They don't know she was nearly killed,
They don't know she lost her mother and father,
They don't know her brother was lost,
They don't know her sister was shot,
They don't know she fled Syria,
They just see an ordinary girl.

Dead or Alive, Who Cares?

Anna-Natasha

If he looks at me before the end of break, he's going to shoot me.

It sounds extreme but he will.

Ever since I stepped foot in high school, he's been looking at me in a way that creates a huge bomb in my skull and I feel like the world is going to disappear right that second.

It's like he knows my past. It's like he knows my plans. What should I do?

I can't stop the bomb I am planning to explode. I can't let him win. Unless,

Unless he is secretly on my side. What if he is?

I don't want to reveal too much.

Maybe he's normal, maybe that's just how normal people look at other normal people.

But I just have this absurd feeling that someone's whispering in my ear, telling me to do something I don't want to do. What should I do if he looks at me before the end of break and doesn't shoot me?

Does that mean he's on my side? Does that mean I've been wrong all this time?

I don't know. Life is confusing.

I'm not sure if this world is suitable for me to live in anymore.

Grass Stains

Nafia

I hope we love each other just like this for the longest time
I hope that we'll all die pretty and full of regrets and I hope
    that my hands are reaching for you
in the dirt somewhere
Even if we're not in the same burial site
                                        Or even in the same universe

I want you to be so good.   I want you to forgive yourself.

One day
I'll ask you, *Where did you put all that love you had for me?*
And you'll say, *Downstairs, dear. In the cupboard next to the bin* and
    I'll go check to see if it's there
and I'll open the cupboard and find only a dead thing. An
    empty thing.

I am eternally in your possession. Front door. Bathroom.
    Orange juice stain.
I remember
being loved by you and what it did to me. I swallowed you. In
    my body I had this rotten dirty
thing and I took it out
    chewed it up
                    I'll let you be fragile and hollow. I'll let myself
touch you how the grass touches you. Barely there.
Truth is I eat dirt and call it care. I kiss the concrete. I rip out
    my own elbow-bone.

I've been doing things to impress you. I've
been doing things.

Like you've dared me to.

Let's pull back my skin shall we? See what lives inside? I bleed
want.

I bleed grass stains.

Kitchen downstairs I yell, *Where did you put the forgiveness?*
You tell me you threw it out. I wonder, dearest, why didn't
you keep some for yourself?

Heat and Shade

Matt

When commuters steamed
On sweaty seats
Like currants in a pud,
You swam freely
In a lightless lake,
Shaded by a wood.
When tracks expanded,
Trains slowed down
Or stopped running altogether.
You were moored in a tranquil cove,
Enjoying milder weather.
When everyone was scorched with heat,
Grass turned brown and dry,
Someone built you solid walls,
Protection from the sky.

Bumper Cars

Josh

'You ready yet, Boyo?'

The raspy voice of my dad bellows from downstairs. I close my door, put my headphones on and drown into the sound of the drums.

I scan my posters: 'The Wombats: Beautiful People Ruin Your Life', 'Greta Van Fleet: From The Fires' and my favourite one, a picture of me and my sister. Before the accident.

That day, we snuck out of the house without Dad noticing and went to the arcade. We spent so much money on the dance machine and the bumper cars. I came out with a few scratches that day. We had a few quid left, so we went into the photo booth and then got milkshakes. Man, those milkshakes were nasty.

We got home and you said you'd lost the photos. I don't think I'd ever screamed at you like that before. I can remember seeing your eyes fill with tears and your chin quiver. I felt so guilty.

Turns out, you'd planned it all along, you just didn't expect me to flip out as much as I did.

I didn't speak to you for so long. They were the only memories we had had for that day and I wanted to keep them because usually we never got along.

A few months later you were admitted to the hospital. No one told me. They just said that you went to sleep at a friend's house for a few weeks.

I missed you so much for those weeks. I just wanted you to come home. You didn't even answer my texts apart from that one time: *Can't text right now, Broski. Love you lots and don't forget that xxx.*

I was confused because you'd never sent me a message like that before, but I smiled so much and read it over and over.

A few days later, Dad came into my room. He looked broken and stank of whisky. He just sat on my bed and didn't move for a good few minutes, then said, 'Put your coat on.'

He didn't tell me where we were going, but then we arrived outside the hospital and I put two and two together.

We walked into your 'room' and everything started to fall apart. You handed me something wrapped in penguin wrapping-paper and you watched a tear splash onto one of the black and white birds.

I know you wanted to cry too, but you had to stay strong in front of me. There was a note written on the outside, not in yours or Dad's writing, so it must've been one of the nurses, which read: *Open When I'm Gone.* If it had been you, you would've added some funny joke or something.

I didn't see you again after that day. I only heard that you'd passed when Dad was talking to Nan. He never told me directly.

I remember sitting in my room, holding the penguin-wrapped present, trying my best not to cry.

Eventually, I opened it.

The pictures from the arcade photo booth fell out. I sat there, staring at them for what felt like hours, wishing you were with me. I turned them over and saw a note on the back, this time in your writing for sure.

Hey Broski, I'm sorry I kept this from you, but I wanted to hang onto these for a while to remember the best bits of my life. I'm sorry I can't be with you anymore. Just remember that I'll always love you and always be with you, no matter where you are. Make sure you keep these pictures safe, and don't let your mates get their grubby hands on them, you know what they're like. I've got to go now, dude. Love you, Joshie − Chloe xxxxx.

Chapter 1 – 'To Think or not to Think'

Romina

6.30 in the morning is an interesting time of the day. It is the time when it is neither dark nor light but it's always cold. It is the sort of time when you can hear nothing outside the window except the occasional passing of a car or any other contraption that was intended to take the human body from one place to another. It is a time no one really wants to be awake and it was the time when Elliot's alarm rang like any other day.

Elliot liked to think. She often thought about life's meaning, like she was some sort of ancient philosopher who had nothing better to do other than think about life rather than going out and actually experiencing it like a normal and sane person would do.

Who are you to judge? would reply the critic that was her brain.

Today, she wanted to think about stress, its history and how it would lead up to the exact moment of her thinking about it. Who taught her what stress was? No one looked into her brain, understood the feeling and said, 'Yep, that's definitely stress.'

What if the feeling was something else? What if happiness was stress and stress was happiness?

Elliot got stressed thinking about stress at exactly 6.32 a.m. and made her way to the dark kitchen where her pills sat patiently waiting for her to pop them out of their place and take them. Elliot thought about how the pills were feeling inside her stomach while making her way to the bathroom. Had she successfully separated any of the chemical families from each other?

How terrible of her.

What went on between Elliot and the bathroom is none of

your business. All I will tell you is that it took from 6.36 a.m. to exactly 7.17 a.m.

By 7.18, Elliot had packed her bag and dressed for the day in different shades of black.

By 7.35 she had finished her breakfast and attempted (failed) to socialise with other humans on social media.

How ironic.

She thought about that until 7.45 a.m. and then stepped out of her brother's insignificant apartment.

Elliot was ready to start the day.

Gunshots

Dijedona

I wake up to the sound of gunshots. Life has just got harder.

Panicked parents are trying to escape this war zone, but the
enemy has already conquered.

Our house is covered. There is no escape. I can see death at
the door.

A gun is fired and everything goes silent. My family gasp. I see
blood on my hands.

Hot pain in my stomach. I faint.

I see a light. A tunnel. Then all goes dark.

As I open my eyes, I see the sun shining through the blinds in
the room.

I see a letter by my bed, handwritten by my family. Tears fall
and I tremble.

Then, as I open the envelope, and before I have the chance to
read it, someone takes it out of my hand and starts running
away.

The person seemed familiar, but I am so tired, my eyes
just close
again.

Ambitionist

Teodor

Jimaphy, a boy with two names, slashed
like the high-energy protein smoothie he drank
just before he jumped over the cliff.
The high energy that was built up inside him
would make his little twelve-year-old heart explodo-burst.
His lungs were accelerating gradually,
but somehow rapidly,
until the grand, gracious moment of his climaxful jump
that would lead to the −
No, not now. He has to build speed.
Aunt Georgia looks at him with the twist of care.
He leaps off the sandy hill. Aunt Georgia sees her nephew
screaming out the adrenaline flowing through his youthful body.
And like that, a picture scene, slow motion,
as if everything stopped.
Everybody knew about the amazing split.
He was training for weeks, his cousin was thinking during the
    moment.
The thud was heard.
The split is done
Like the gymnast he is to this day.

My Biggest Regret

Alise

As I walk past you, my eyes don't leave the early morning raindrops that glisten on the window.

Butterflies appear in my stomach as I catch a glimpse of you like it's the first time it has ever happened.

You turn your head to me and smile, but I don't think you realise it's me.

That may have just been a brief pleasure but it will forever be a memory.

'It's my fault.' A thought I can't push away.

'It's my fault.' The words wander at the back of my head.

My eyes run along the dusty windowsills.

It's been one year since you went, yet I feel like I've lived a thousand.

My eyes roam across the hallway, half expecting you to be there, but I know you won't be. They've tried talking to me.

They said you went to a better place and I want to believe that, I do, but I can't.

I need you to be **here**.

I'm selfish. I was selfish. I broke your heart and couldn't tell you why.

You wouldn't understand me, I said to myself, yet now, that's my biggest regret,

A risk I wish I'd taken.

I didn't love you more than I loved myself.

'It's my fault.' I've come to realise

That thought is here to stay.

Rainy Afterday

Scarlett

I would love to admit that I didn't look back, but then,
That would be a lie.
I looked back.
More than once.

Even through the misty windows of the bus I glanced back.
Veins of vapour mussed up the scene,
Scrawled up along the pane, but still,
My eyes couldn't help it.

Something Freudian, something about the human condition,
    maybe.
I don't even understand it myself.

Maybe in the Bible Lot's wife didn't turn into a pillar of salt
    when she spared her biting, burning city a final farewell.
Eyes brushing over the smoking spires, charred cathedrals,
A lilting look, like the quiver of a violin string.

Maybe it was the seawater tears?
Maybe she trembled and became like stone.
Maybe she shuddered, with the look that salted her wounds,
    and hardened over.
You know how they are with their metaphors.
I don't know much about scripture, but I do know that.

I read somewhere that boiling saltwater summons the smell of
     a storm, something like the ozone, crackling lightning, the
     warped twigs of a tree making black smears in the sky,
     clacking in the wind.
I read somewhere that, when it's boiled, only a very fine
     residue remains: powdery, like ground sand.

I dab the tip of my finger with the tip of my tongue, quick, fast,
     a flickering snake fork.
You need to take it gently: press the digit into the salt-sand,
     leave a dune imprint.
I think it tastes like my tears.

Yesterday I spent so long crying, the tears dried and, when I
     licked my lips, they were the sea.
It was funny: I thought I'd tilted my head back, so they ran
     trenches into my hair.

Funny, how you lose track of tears.
But when eyes are lost marbles,
Mine are disobedient and roll all over the place.
Somehow, it seems, they can't help but rivet
On you.

Chapter 2 – 'Creep, Much?'

Romina

Elliot needed watching, her mother insisted on it.

The bottom right of the CCTV states the day, date and the time, 8.10 a.m.

The room is the perfect balance of light and dark.

One window, the one on the far right, is open. It is the only source of air, causing the curtains to swing back and forth as if they are possessed. The computers are turned off, untouched.

The tables are filled with papers and folders, the chairs are all over the place and there is noise, lots of noise, from outside the room.

One table has no folders on it, just a tray filled with hand sanitisers inside broken teacups.

Its colour is suspicious.

The bulletin boards announce everything you need to know about university life but nothing about the students. Except one drawing.

The room is empty besides Elliot.

Memories like a Snapshot

Aseel

As I look at you, I smile.
As I close my eyes, I twitch.
As I take a deep breath, I turn the page.
It's you, younger than you ever looked.
I remember, as I stroke your thick black hair
That covers your eyes,
Your handsome outfit with that splendid tie.
I always loved the way you smiled at me,
I thought I'd always see your eyes twinkling at me
But no, it was my imagination of you now.
My eyes start to tear up
I know I have to close you up
And put you away.
RIP Grandad,
I love you.
xoxo

You Can only Create it

Azim

'People think you can buy, steal, lose and create memories. But in truth, you can only do one of those. You can only create them.

'If you can steal and/or lose and/or buy memories, then you should solve or at least try to solve riddles daily to strengthen your mind. The point is, they are not real enough, they are not strong enough; you can only create them.'

– Ahmad Al-Ghazali II

It Starts

Dijedona

It starts with the Soviets building a wall.

Barbed wire is put in its place. People try to escape to the Allies' side.

Deaths take place. Families are separated. Will they ever be reunited? – Erm, yeah.

Hi, my name is Elizabeth. My parents are writers, just like their parents before them, all the way back to 100 AD. I have been constantly pressured to write stories and essays since I was a young child. I hate it.

My dreams have never been heard. My future is blurred as I don't know what to do. Everyone's eyes are always watching me. I feel like the people on the Soviet side of the wall. Life feels like a prison, because it is.

They don't know why I am sitting in the corner. Not even my best friends.

When I sit in a corner no one knows I exist; well, that's what I wish could happen.

I wish people thought I didn't exist.

Alec

Kayana

The park was normally a place where I could go to get everything off my mind.

A place to feel free, especially when it is empty and I feel like I own it all. Just for me.

But this time it was different. It wasn't my friendly rainy day, but strange and tingly.

No matter how hard I tried to feel free, I couldn't get Alec out of my head.

I sat down and began writing in my journal to get my feelings out, but I couldn't think straight.

I got up to pack my things. Hell, I couldn't even stand straight. One thing kept popping into my mind. Alec.

Lost in my thoughts, I felt a warm body lean against my back. I didn't need to turn around to know it was him.

I dropped my bag.

He pulled aside my raincoat collar and kissed my neck in the cold heavy rain.

I pulled up my bitter hood and took a step away from him.

'Don't think you can just walk back into my life and try to make things better; you can't kiss this wound away,' I said, as I picked up my bag and quietly walked out of the park with only one thing on my mind.

Alec.

You

Harriet

I know your face
Your eyes softly sad
Please don't do what my dad did
Don't sit there and fade away to grey

THE HAND

Reinhardas

The End was near…

The Moon shattered into tiny pieces as the gigantic laser beam came towards the Earth.

It shone as brightly as the sun. Was it over? Was Earth destined for this tragic fate?

Millions of people were running in all directions, seeking shelter before the laser hit… But one man stood there, staring at the laser. 'What is he doing?' I thought, in utter confusion.

Suddenly, the man kneeled down and positioned his hands together. It seemed that he was praying for God.

The Cellophane Boy

Sarah

The cellophane boy sat at the corner
Someone asked him a question
He answered
No one was listening
Why would they?
They had never done it before
The cellophane boy wondered why no one ever spoke to him
He lived in the same area as them
Ate the same food, sat in the same classes
What was so wrong with him?
The cellophane boy was soon informed
'You're the ugliest person ever,' they said
'Your face is disgusting,' they said
They didn't know how their sharp words had sentenced
    his death
The next day the cellophane boy didn't turn up to school
No one noticed
His disappearance meant nothing to them
It was in assembly they were told
The children were silent, but they couldn't grieve
They had paid no interest to him before
Their only memory of him was his name
The cellophane boy.

Eden

Ayah

The dog is running. My eyes are focused. I break the ray of concentration for half a second to see Eden slowly creeping closer.

With every step, his bony legs slide, creaking against the floorboard, mine scrunch to my chest.

After what just happened, I don't think he'll ever be my Eden again: the brother who took me under his wing, showed me how to misbehave, or the friend who played my games even though he always hated them. He comes closer and then he stops.

He leans in. I feel his breath brush against my cheeks. The blood on his white football shirt stains my knees.

He raises a finger to his lips and one soft breath splashes out of his mouth like a gentle wave.

Chapter 3 – 'Dude, That's Deep...'

Romina

Elliot was feeling melancholic today. Ha, when does she not? No, but seriously. She was feeling think-y.

She was writing her thoughts. It was what her therapist told her to do.

Fine, fine. Don't beg. This is what she wrote:

'Time has an absurd effect on the mind. When we're five, we want the simple things in life like staying up a few minutes after bedtime or having the newest toys. At ten, we become ambitious and want to achieve the impossible, like going to Hogwarts or visiting Area 51. At fifteen, ambition dies and all that matters is school, exams... God I want a break! At thirty, we want happiness, money, a good life... death.'

What is Love?

Alise

As I trudge ahead, I can hear the ice cracking underfoot like
    breaking glass.
A grim flashback comes to mind: us quarrelling like the tides
    against a cliff.
I feel the tears like two wet flies crawling down my cheeks.
I remember your eyes, wicked   as life itself,
Your grip so tight your knuckles shone white.
I guess that's what love is,
A nightmare of suffering.
Yet
I love you more than I've ever loved myself.
Crushed with sorrow,
Tinged with regret.

A Strong Desire for Something to Happen

Madalena

He looked out the window of the old cabin, staring up at the
    darkness that surrounded him.
He moved the latch and slid the glass up,
the cold wind blasting into his face,
the full moon shining down on him,
encouraging him to lift his leg up and step out into the cruel,
    dark night,
to stop waiting for his spaceship to take him up to heaven.
He entered the world,
guarded by a few twinkling stars that poked holes through the
    blanket that was the sky.

Memories to Ashes

Josh

There it stands. The nostalgia. The horror.

It is falling apart. How dreadful, yet thankful.

I loved this place, sometimes at least.

My whole childhood was wasted in this place but now I am so grateful for it. I hated it. I miss it.

I always wanted it taken away, but now that it's gone it feels as if half my life has gone with it. I take one more look, a private photograph, then walk through the gate.

I stand on something, a sign. I thought it had been taken away with all the other riches in this place. The sign is charred and melted but you can still just about make out the words 'Academy' and 'Primary' with two arrows pointing in opposite directions. The beautiful greenery. The rose bush and the hanging pots of cyclamen. All gone.

I remember them so clearly, but now they have been replaced with the dark black ground full of fragile ash. Empty cans of Coke and beer litter the floor where the wooden gazebo used to be. Ah, the memories I had in that thing with my friends. Gone.

And soon so will be the memories.

I never realised how much I would miss this place.

I love it. I hated it. I wanted it gone and now...

I want it back.

The Circle of Us

Iman

How is it possible to be so useless?
How can I feel so lost in the place I call home?
I called you my friend
My love
I thought you felt it too
Bubbles fill the air, sending me floating in a pool of questions
That rose scent, that oh-so-familiar *once upon a time*
Was it fake from the beginning?
Did this mean nothing to you?
There must have been something
Anything
Please let me cling on to the hope that I ever meant something
    to you
Remember the small gestures, your warm hand painting small
    circles on my palm
I thought they were circles of love
Weren't they circles of love?
Your soft voice I was so fond of is all but a distant memory
Lost
Help me remember
Come back
I should be better than that
But I'm not
Say the word, I'll be there
Waiting from the heartbreak, clinging on to those moments
Here goes the circle
The circle of us.

Gone

Anna-Natasha

I don't know what to do besides posting pictures of my mum.

I thought it would help me but it didn't.

Every day since she passed I feel less like myself, as if I get further away with every breath I take.

When Mum was alive she was able to shine through the cloud that followed me everywhere.

I miss her.

I wish I could just wake up and she would be there.

Jack is only four, so he doesn't even know what life is. He just sits down, kissing our newborn brother. When he finds out that Mum died giving birth, he will cry for the rest of his life.

I am only ten, so I don't think I'm old enough to look after the whole house, including our dog. I think our dog is the only one who knows how I feel. She keeps on coming to me, her ears drooping, looking all upset. As the days go past, the cloud circles me, trying to take control. I struggle. I won't let it win. Not yet.

My Saturday Night

Nina

Tummy rumbles
Grab an oversized blanket
Take my earphones out
Turn off phone
Sprint out of bed
'How do I have this much energy?'
Wrapped up
Feet are cold
Heating's off
See my dog
Always awake
Her eyes are red
Staring at the front door
I stumble to the kitchen
See my neighbour
Through the window
Having a party
They're all drunk
I don't understand eighteen-year-old minds
Open fridge
The white bulb blinds me
Grab a cold Capri-Sun
Crap, no straw
I would like a refund
Get some pretzels
Run back to my room
Jump into bed
Cover myself in blankets

I can feel the heat consume my body
Turn on YouTube
Realise its 2.18
I pretend I haven't noticed.

Picture your Best

Nafia

Picture your best
                down the hallway of your favourite building
                      Now picture me in a sundress
Telling you
          I'm tired
Have I ruined it?
              Have I ruined the illusion?
I said there are no words here
            I said there was no truth
                    I told you what my line was

I told you
I am trying to be tender I told you
              I told you
you ask
    me how I am, and I said
craving
THIS IS A STORY ABOUT TENDERNESS
TWO PEOPLE AT A BUS STOP SHOUTING WORDS OF
DISDAIN, like it's so easy to hate
I scream at you down in the dirt   shovel to mouth

And you held your breath while I was in the bathroom,
    washing down my sentiments with the bar of soap I bought
    you
             Last summer
                Down the drain
        Last summer
          Pipe to the ocean

                                    Last summer and
I ask you how you are and you say
Aching
                        Establishing a good relationship with the people you've hurt
   What a line,
        How ridiculous it is to think that you can say it and it
        might be true
Sorry on your mouth well is it really or did it die out
            Will I find your hands in a shallow grave down the
            street
  Big crowd where I cannot see your face
Where
                        I cannot fathom why I would need to
Purity is a myth, darling. Redemption is a story god will tell
   you, smoking in his bedroom.
            There should be a world where we are kind.
Anyway
   I'm running down the bridge yelling
Someone else's name
Laughing
     How stupid I was
                To ever think you were anywhere to be seen.

Brother

Teodor

You want the things I want,
Want to reach the successes
I reach
With my last thrust of emotional grief
But never realise how meaningless they are.
You want to have my skill when you actually
Yourself have double the amount
Of my own.
So much potential and you wasted it to be like
Your older brother.
DON'T.
Look, when I was your age no one showed me
How to do this, how to do deal with that. Taught myself.
But you, I don't want you to follow me
On those stairs with those rusty ancient nails barely hanging.
Be yourself   Not like me.
You can do it, much better, so let's leave it,
Between me and this paper,
You are the talented one.

How We Hid

Harriet

Remember being wrapped in a quilt under the stairs in the dark, with a push-on light stuck to the wall, feeling pillows squashing, seeing glow-in-the-dark stars and old wallpaper forgotten by decorators, peeling away to reveal deeper layers of pastel animals and bulbous flowers, and pencil marks of remembered words and desired phrases curated from books.

Remember the warmth from the pipes running water under the floor, bringing the carpet to life like the fur of a large animal, the whirring, ticking silence, how we hid away and liked it.

Remember when we were young and never even thought of this day.

We Know

Ayah

She creeps up behind you
Meant to be a gift of god

A golden creation
A sense of magic
But when she chooses you
You don't know why

She tiptoes around you
Careful not to make the floorboards creak
But you feel her breath

Against your neck
You can't escape

You start to run
But she won't go away

No matter how fast
She'll always be there
You feel her hands
Her nails claw into your skin
You turn around
And beg

for her to loosen her grip.

Message

Azim

This is the act of a heart beating,
releasing blood from the pulmonary artery with oxyhaemoglobin
attached to four oxygen atoms and nutrients being transported
through antagonistic muscles;
Microscopic sensory neurons taking electrical pulses through
the body, the central nervous system, making the same journey
back, but with a message...
'WAKE UP!'

After Ophelia Hit the Bank

Scarlett

The bank of a scrawled meander winds like a slack noose.

It is crowned by a grove, each prong of the firs studding the fringe where the water meets mud and congeals into a stiff scab edging the creeping roots.

The river is one of many tributaries, forgotten as the Ock or Evenlode, and runs knowing no one will question a misplaced current, critique the upflowing water, or ask about the wet heap flung against the rhizomes that are slowly having their way with her, tentative tendrils gradually feeling their way around the hump of a hipbone, the hollow of a ribcage.

The twilight illuminates the most glorious things: sprouting spears of reeds, the russet of hair, lilies dappling the slower regions of the river like dabs of paint on a swirling canvas. It limns the waxen leaves and dances over the shadows in the tree bark, empty eye sockets, spangles over the dimples in the water-face. It reaches with heavy, unchecked fingers towards the tender underbelly of the river, but silt stirs and rears a warning head, and the light is diluted.

Just like that, it snatches back questing hands, retreating to a point over the treetops, winking its last at the river, who churns and snarls a scowl in inky sand.

A new force seems to muster: you wouldn't have guessed they had been holding their breaths, too small to be noticed.

These tiny motes of dust, these gilded clusters, slices of bioluminescence, rise from nowhere and everywhere.

They ebb and flow, pulse and throb.

These silent exchanges of dilate and recoil, monitored by no one and nothing, but they are unafraid.

Their filaments flicker, and a tiny noctambulist flies a lazy circle.

He lands on the white wrist of a widow of the river, slumped, half-submerged beneath the water, and she makes no move to wave off the curious glow.

A crust of years-old mud saturates her tattered gown, speckles her perfect, sunken face.

Sun-blasted and slack, she is utterly hollow, a Halfling of the river and the land, some neglected nymph, Olympus's plaything, cast aside from spite.

Laughable, that she would lie cold and limp, deflated as a lung that huffs a breath of air.

Absurd, that her blood would desert her veins, mingle with the knotweed and water-crowfoot, leave her drained as an unstoppered bottle.

A passive amphibian, she sits and watches the night meld into the day, the sun swivel and the moon glisten, a parchment skull never frowning, never smiling, only an observer amongst this, lapping blanket pulled up to her chin, pillows a sprawling thicket of roots.

She never reached the sea.

candy dream aesthetics

Jenni

candy dream aesthetics
dancing into view
dreams lost, perverted
soft uwu desires turned away
cut away,
sacrifice me and
we'll see your truth,
four horses carry each
their own burden
tear down the castles,
rip apart the churches
reveal god
in their pure foetal state
perverted, ruined chaos
uwu uwu uwu it away.
pastel angel cuteness
so *kawaii*, such a lie.
parents always argue
can't they just divorce.
can't i ever even
go back?
albino ghost dears
plague my eyes
cut them out
now

Mystery in Maysville

Sonny

It was the same old day at school. His eyes almost out of their sockets, glued to his face, the upside-down grin meeting his upside-down grin. The difference was, however, that Jim never smiled; at least that's what everybody thought because nobody knew what happened at the end of the street with no name. If he sat at the end of his bed waiting for something, crying, or if he sat down with his family and played a board game, nobody knew and that's the way it had been for the last 150 years.

Jim had a pale face with almost no colour, except for his eyes which nested deep, watching every human being they met. His hair, blacker than soot, went from the top of his head and stopped halfway at the back. This was unknown to people because his head was covered by a hat that was never removed. On this hat were the words: *MFC 1915–1916 champions.*

This was what shocked people the most in the town of Maysville. The Maysville Football Club 1915–1916 champions went missing after going on a walk. Nobody knew what had happened and they were never found again. Rumours emerged that they had gone missing after walking alongside the field that belonged to the Revanells. The Revanells were Jim's family and that was the year 1935.

Jim sat at the back of a classroom with cold and damp walls. A class where the air was considered to be 95% asbestos and 5% carbon dioxide. Mould was left for educational purposes, left for the students to watch and the mould to spread. There were five people in the class who made Jim's stomach boil and teeth grind, but he showed no sign of this to anybody.

Tom, the popular one; Barney, the not very intelligent one;

Sally, the clever one; Hucklebury, the bully; and Sid, the rich one. Jim only got off his seat once the hand-rung bell went and he would sit under a tree, reading a book dating back to 1850.

The year 1935, the year of the bad harvest, and Jim deprived of dry meat, rye bread and tomatoes...

The book was called *The Causes and Effects of the Bad Harvest – 1550 to 1850*. The author's name was J.R.M Revanell, who was found dead from suicide soon after its publication.

In the year 1934, villagers claimed they had seen Mr Revanell walking into the forest with a long blade. The forest, which no one had set foot in for almost twenty years. The last people to go in were the police.

The year after that, people claimed they had seen Mr Revanell walking into the forest with the same blade. Although this time he was smaller.

Find Yourself

Nina and Alise

Hello,
You don't know who I am
I've been watching over you
I've seen the sick things you've done
Neglecting the people who care for you
The way you suffer inside
The way you rot your own mind
    say you're fine
The way you crumble your feelings
    turn down your thoughts
The way you don't know how to stop when you start
Look at you
A lost soul in the found place
Trapped in a puzzle where you're the piece that's missing
If only you could find
Yourself…

Online Rage

Reinhardas

It was 9 p.m. on a Tuesday and I logged on to my computer to play an online video game. The server was packed with new players, but I was fine with that. There were four remaining players for me to eliminate so I was happy, or I was until I got shot.

The person who did it was NOT friendly. He was counting the number of people he killed as if they were just numbers and was always saying 'EZ' which is rude to say to other gamers who are trying their best. He then complained about how his computer is laggy when he gets killed.

What should I do? I wondered. Reporting in this game isn't an option since it never works. Leaving the server makes me feel like I didn't complete my objective to achieve justice. So what now?

I decided on a new option. It was to make him rage-quit! The next round, I managed to get him and then the next round again and again and again. Soon enough, he left, typing his goodbye…

'I *hate* you.'

I Am Not a Human Being

Madalena

I look out of the window of my spaceship as I leave   you
standing on the ground looking back
at me,

getting smaller and smaller as I fly off into the universe

and leave you on your world.

I am making my way
to new places
to find new faces
and meet new races

But still my heart is heavy

There are inhabitants on your planet

But   I   am   all   alone   on   my   spaceship,

until I dock on another world

and again pretend that I am part of their life,

pretend that I belong there

but I don't.

I am not a human being.

What's the Point?

Dijedona

I don't want to write
I can't think of anything
I don't know
Why am I here?
I want to be in the book
He's so annoying
I can't think
No one listens   No one ever has
But I just have to do it
No choice
Get on with life
Roll my eyes every time I hear a voice
Mind blank
People shouting at me but   I can't hear a single thing
What do I do?
Help me
Help me fight my mind

DEMONS

Iman

D ying inside, my walls crumbling to useless ash

E very look, sound, action, twists, squeezing out something
negative. Always something negative

M oments of misery inflicted upon my aching body

O bliterating every ounce of positivity, scared of my own
darkness, lost in my maze

N eglecting the fact that there might be hope waiting
somewhere in the abyss

S laughtering my angels

The Walk to DETENTION

Aseel

I get up gingerly,
Knowing I have to walk the walk of shame,
My teacher grasping the phone, dialling 300 (as usual).
My best friend gasps, and laughs turn into disappointment.
I feel annoyed and want to **INTIMIDATE** the teacher
So I walk angrily to the door and open it, but as I open the
  door I remember I have an appointment.
I just want to turn back time and **REBELLLLL!**
But you know I can't do anything about it (as usual).
I know that my mum will be angry but my dad won't care.
I slam the door and wait for someone to 'collect me'.
The wait is tedious and very long (like, verrrrryyyy long)…
He comes out and tells me to go to the cafeteria.   I do.
Walking along the corridor it feels like I can hear
One million voices,
Voices telling me to rebel.   I carry on walking.
I go down the stairs and every step is a punishment,
My heart feels like an axe is chopping at it every second.
I go to the line and say my name and why I'm here.
I say it's a 'behaviour' and that it's not my fault (as usual).
I enter…
It's going to be a long night…

The Kiss

Kayana

364 days,
20 hours,
16 minutes,
28 seconds.
Finally there you were.
For a long time we stood there
Embracing, and nothing mattered but the sheer comfort of
    your body against mine,
Your familiar smell, your warmth and vitality.
The way you soothe me, feeling your smooth hands run
    through my hair.
Your enchanting honeyed scent lures me to pull myself closer
    to you.
Your harbour of adoration consoles our love.   Our heads
    turn to one another.
Your playful smirk flushes my cheeks with blush.
Your provoking lips stride,
Interlocking our flame of internal love with,
The kiss.

The People Who Said What

Anna-Natasha

The man who said, '*The trouble is, now children are being raised by phones.*'

The TV covered the room. Screens were overpopulating the brain. Sadness was about to become permanent. Children were becoming dumber. People became lonelier.

However, one person called Anton Green loved technology.

He told everyone that he had created all technology. But one day, people found out who actually created technology, so now he is very unpopular and rejects what he said and hates it all.

The children said, '*Look at him.*'

The class were shouting at this one boy. He was lonely as hell, both of his parents were gone. He had promised himself he would not do the same.

The boy lived with his two aunties called Jude and Kate. They weren't the kindest of people. They kept on saying to him, 'You don't belong here.'

In school, people said, 'Look at him! Why is he always so sad?'

They had no idea at all.

Scan

Matt

Currants hung like lanterns
Quinces like church bells
We saw the doctor lady
Who said that all was well.

We filled ourselves with Turkish food
Munched crispy strips of bread
We smiled with reassurance
At what the doctor lady said.

Apples large as grapefruit

Pears like joyful tears
We smiled because the doctor lady
Put away our fears.

saturday hunger

Jenni

i'm hungry for happiness
but the big gods don't care
the tree-hugger wished for love
but the mirror didn't think it fair
these sweet dreams would taste sweeter
without the chants of   **[Do It]**   behind them
on the way out please keep your fake love and
discard your pursuit of happiness

The Fates of a Thatcher's Eighties

Scarlett

The Fates of a Thatcher's eighties sit on a crumbling wall. The idle chalk-lines of a childhood spent in boredom trace the bricks, pausing where the cement seeps out, long since crusted over, stale bread. It is summer, and their skin shines a healthy, hot sheen. One smells of chamomile, the other of chlorine, and the last of cocoa butter. The mesh of their scents flits in the breeze that carries the phlegmy coughs of car exhaust-pipes too far from the road.

They are waiting.

Maybe trying to whittle away a summer in the city, where the glass and steel of the sleeping giants refract the light, magnifying it in a way that makes the neck itch and skin prickle.

Maybe they are poised.

Their slumped shoulders, up-tilted heads, flickering eyelids, all seem to contest this.

But their hands are clenched, furled up tight, white-knuckled, blind puppy dogs.

The laziness, languishing on this wall, lilting like a fat bee tracing circles in the air, shutters with the sound of newly-soled shoes on the pavement.

Small steps scuff away the newness, hopping along, and slowly they come to a halt.

The Fates are watching.

The locks of the fists of their hands unlatch.

A thread, two blades from the same pair of scissors.

Maybe this little boy knows.

He almost certainly does not.

He does not know the tumour in his lung has reached out

with feeling tendrils, deathly roots caressing his arteries.

He is healthy, if a tad pale, his mother thought, for the London summer.

Besides, he has asthma.

He's usually a little short of breath, the poor thing.

Chamomile holds the threat taut.

Chlorine has the left blade, cocoa butter the right.

His game of hopscotch draws to a close.

A flash of light

The penny drops

The thread is cut.

Vintage

Josh

As the man walks up his creaky stairs, a groan comes from the attic, another slat has come out of place. The crackling of the record player makes itself heard over Frank Sinatra's voice.

The rustic hunting rifle hangs over his bed on bent screws. He takes the record off and lets the crackle play as if it can't be heard. He opens the warped and half-hinged cupboard.

He has three sets of clothes: a cheap suit passed down from his dad, nightwear, and work clothes he doesn't wear any more. He reaches into the top corner of the cupboard and grabs a blue box full of multicoloured capsules. One... two... three... four... One by one. Nine... ten... With every pill, his face shows more disgust than the last. He closes the box and struggles to put it back; as he finally manages to, he strains his back.

The record player goes off and he lies down, placing his dentures in a glass of water.

He stays in the same position as always, due to the crater in his rusty-spring bed, making it harder and harder to get out in the morning.

Mind the Gap

Sarah

Train?

Nope. Only a light in the tunnel. What's the time? Uh-oh. Five
  minutes left.

The stuffy breath on my neck is making me extremely
  uncomfortable.

One centimetre forward and I'm on the tracks, one centimetre
  back and I'm on top of somebody's shoes.

I don't want a detention. I want a voucher at the end of the
  year. No!

Everyone is going to look at me when I arrive, and rub my
  detention in my face.

I will have no pride. This cannot be happening. Wait, a tube!

It's full. I'm going to start hyperventilating soon.

                                    Just breathe, Sarah.

It'll be okay.

Apple Core Decay

Lola

Rainbow-striped throw
white sheet
open window
blue curtains
Cigarette lazily smokes itself out
You aren't here
but she is
It seems she can't leave this place
she loves it
really
Yesterday she was here again
and she missed you
again
But there was something off
It sounds silly
but the blanket was made the other way
and why was it vertical?
She couldn't understand
she had to remake it
I think she doesn't want this place
to change

BIOGRAPHIES

ANNA-NATASHA ANDERSEN: 'Be Alright' by Dean Lewis

MADALENA MARCAL WHITTLES: 'Drop the World' by Lil Wayne

ASEEL TARIQ OSMAN: NSG 'Options'

HUGH KINDRED: 'Rock Your Baby', *Fantastic Mr Fox*, *Black Market*

SONNY BRETT: 'All Along the Watchtower' / 'Killing in the Name' / 'There is a Light that Never Goes Out'

NINA BENTLEY: 'Life on Mars'

ALISE CENAJ: 'Let Her Go'

KAYANA BURKE: *The Hidden Diary of Marie Antoinette*

REINHARDAS GIRDZIUSAS: *The Tanker!*

TEODOR GEROV: 'Waiting in the Wings'

MATT REVEL: *Why? Here's Why?*

LOLA STOKES: 'For a Minute' by Joy Crookes

NAFIA TAHAR: 'South London Forever' by Florence and the Machine

IMAN SALEH: *Valerie* meets *All The Bright Places*

DIJEDONA MALETTA: 'Dionysus'

JOSHUA WHITELOCK: 'Through the Valley' meets *Indiana Jones*

HARRIET LACEY: '80 Windows'

AYAH KASSHA: *I'm A Celebrity Get Me Out of Here*

AZIM OS-MAN: *The Curious Incident of the Dog in the Night-Time*

JENNI MITCHELL: 'I Hate Everyone' and 'Uncle' by Mindless Self Indulgence

SARAH IDUNDUN: 'Thriller' by Michael Jackson

SCARLETT STOKES: 'Almost (sweet music)' by Hozier

ROMINA AGHAIE: 'Alrighty Aphrodite' by Peach Pit

ACKNOWLEDGEMENTS

Melanie Curtis at Avon DataSet for her overwhelming support for First Story and for giving her time in typesetting this anthology.

Emily Bedford for copy-editing this anthology and supporting the project.

Kate Kunac-Tabinor and all the designers at Oxford University Press for their overwhelming support for First Story, and Fiona MacColl specifically for designing the cover of this anthology.

David Greenwood and Foysal Ali at Aquatint for printing this anthology at a discounted rate.

The William Shelton Education Charity for supporting First Story in this school.

HRH The Duchess of Cornwall, Patron of First Story.

Thanks to:
Arts Council England, Alice Jolly & Stephen Kinsella, Andrea Minton Beddoes & Simon Gray, The Arvon Foundation, BBC Children in Need, Beth & Michele Colocci, Blackwells, Boots Charitable Trust, Brunswick, Charlotte Hogg, Cheltenham Festivals, Clifford Chance, Dulverton Trust, Edith Murphy Foundation, First Editions Club Members, First Story Events Committee, Frontier Economics, Give A Book, Ink@84, Ivana Catovic of Modern Logophilia, Jane & Peter Aitken, John Lyon's Charity, John Thaw Foundation, Miles Trust for the Putney & Roehampton Community, Old Possum's Practical Trust, Open Gate Trust, Oxford University Press, Psycle Interactive,

Royal Society of Literature, Sigrid Rausing Trust, The Stonegarth Fund, Teach First, Tim Bevan & Amy Gadney, Walcot Foundation, Whitaker Charitable Trust, William Shelton Education Charity, XL Catlin, our group of regular donors, and all those donors who have chosen to remain anonymous.

Most importantly we would like to thank the students, teachers and writers who have worked so hard to make First Story a success this year, as well as the many individuals and organisations (including those who we may have omitted to name) who have given their generous time, support and advice.